Written by

JANE F. COLLEN

Illustrated by

DAVID TRUMBLE

Streamline Brand Associates, Inc.

Print Editions ISBN 978-0-9855732-4-9

Visit www.Enjella.com & www.rumbleart.co.uk for more information

Enjella, the president of the Elbow Fairies, was waiting for her best friend and vice-president, Alicia.

But just like every day,

Alicia could not decide what to wear, or who she wanted to be.

Yesterday she was the captain of a ship.
She had stormed the sea and made
friends with a whale.

Around lunchtime she had felt
more like a mermaid.

In the evening she was an astronaut,
zooming to the moon, past all the stars
and around the comets.

But today?

What did she want to do? Who did she want to be?

The sun summoned her.
The flowers beckoned.
Adventure called.

The dogs distracted her. She
wanted to be a veterinarian-ballerina,
dancing through the park.

But the clouds captivated her!
She felt as regal as the Queen of
her home, Sparkleshire.

And when the wind wildly
whispered to her: COME PLAY,
it made her feel brave and daring.

She wanted to be everything at once -- the choices were overwhelming.

When Enjella knocked on the door
Alicia STILL could not decide what
to wear, or who to be.

Seeing Enjella reminded her . . . It did not matter.
She could be everything her heart desired,
including herself.

Alicia was exactly where
she wanted to be!

The End

About the Author

Jane F. Collen loves to tell stories. The award-winning Enjella® Adventure Series evolved from stories she told her children at bedtime. The Author's favorite pastime is to combine history and magic to create stories with characters who solve real life problems. Mrs. Collen lives in New York.

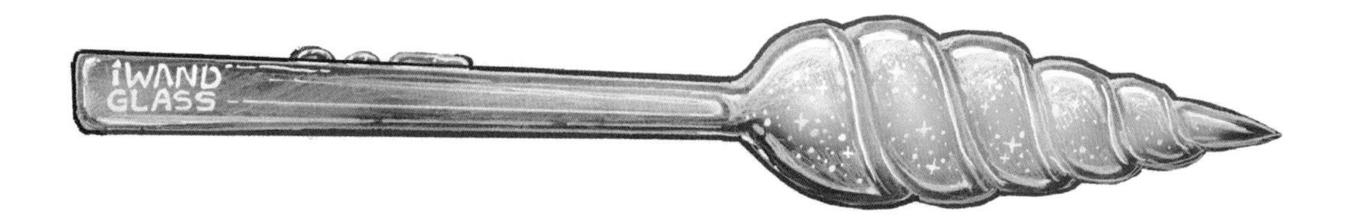

About the Illustrator

David Trumble has a magical capacity to bring characters to life. Doodling and drawing since he was a child, Mr. Trumble's art has been published in newspapers, magazines and books to critical acclaim. He lives in London.

Made in the USA
Lexington, KY
28 February 2015